5/09

MUSEUM TRIP

by **Barbara Lehman**

Houghton Mifflin Company Boston 2006

For Joshua, Sophie, Sam, and Ben

www.houghtonmifflinbooks.com

The illustrations are watercolor, gouache, and ink.

Library of Congress Cataloging-in-Publication Data
Lehman, Barbara.
   Museum trip / by Barbara Lehman.
      p. cm.
Summary: In this wordless picture book, a boy imagines himself inside some of the exhibits when he
goes on a field trip to a museum.
ISBN 0-618-58125-1 hardcover
[1. School field trips—Fiction. 2. Museums—Fiction. 3. Stories without words.] I. Title.
PZ7.L52176Mus 2006   [E]—dc22   2005052840

ISBN-13: 978-0-618-58125-2

Printed in China
SCP 10 9 8 7 6 5 4 3 2

fig. 104. 8

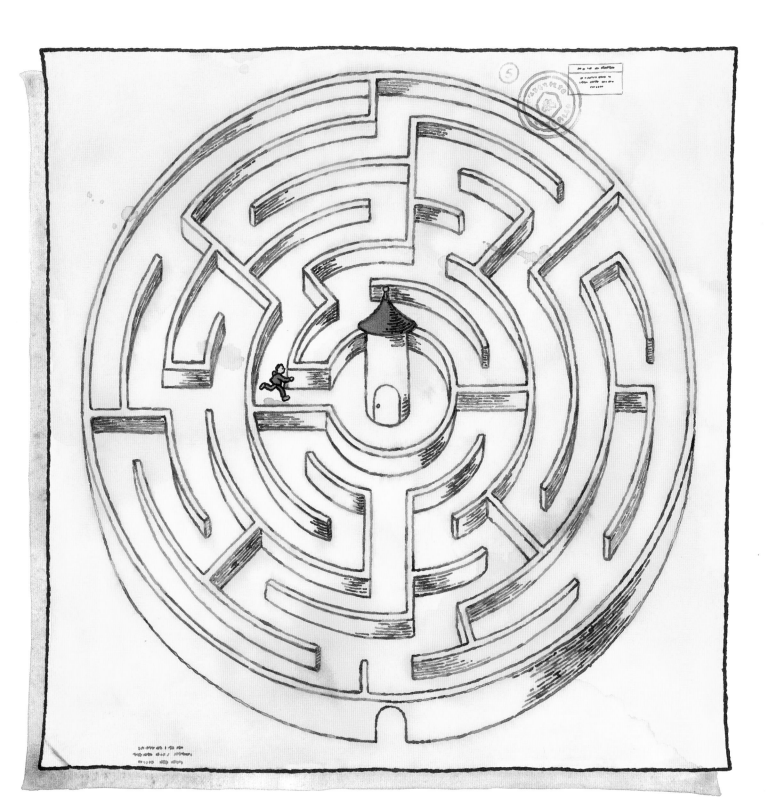